Jennifer's Rabbit

by **Tom Paxton**

illustrated by **Elizabeth Miles**

HarperCollinsPublishers

To Jennifer
—T.P.

To Charlie
—E.M.

Jennifer slept in her little bed
With dreams of her rabbit in her little head.
Jennifer's rabbit, brown and white,
Left the house and ran away one night,

Along with a turtle and a kangaroo,
And seventeen monkeys from the city zoo....

And Jennifer too.

They ran through the forest
And they all held hands.

They came to the ocean
With the cookie-crumb sands.
They called it the sea
Of the very best dreams,
And they all built a castle
Of the best moonbeams
And Milky Way streams.

And there on the sands where the starfish play,
The ship sailed in from the moonbeam bay.

They all went sailing on the starlight sea,

Where they all had cookies
With oolong tea....

And Jenny had three.

They danced on the decks of the red-sailed brig.
The monkeys and the sailors did a whirling jig.
Turtle played the fiddle and the rabbit played kazoo,

And they bowed to each other
As polite folks do....

And Jenny bowed too.

Then, "My," said the turtle
As the clock struck three,
"The hour is growing very late for me."
"Not at all," said the rabbit,
"And I'll tell you why.

We still haven't counted
Every star in the sky...."

Said Jenny, "Let's try."

So they counted on the ship
And they counted on the shore.

They counted through the forest to the bedroom door.

They counted in bed till they could count no more.
Then they all fell asleep, and the final score
Was a trillion and four.

Yes, the rabbit and the turtle and the kangaroo
And Jenny fell asleep as sleepy folk do.

Just like you....

Jennifer's Rabbit

Text copyright © 1967, 1969 by SBK U Catalog, Inc.

Illustrations copyright © 2001 by Elizabeth Miles

Printed in the United States of America.

www.harperchildrens.com

Library of Congress Cataloging-in-Publication Data
Paxton, Tom, date. Jennifer's rabbit / by Tom Paxton ;
    illustrated by Elizabeth Miles.   p.   cm.
Summary: Jennifer dreams that she, a rabbit, a turtle, a
kangaroo, and seventeen monkeys visit the ocean with
the cookie-crumb sands. ISBN 0-688-15262-7
        ISBN 0-06-029216-4 (lib. bdg.)
        [1. Dreams—Fiction.   2. Bedtime—Fiction.
        3. Animals—Fiction.   4. Stories in rhyme.]
            I. Miles, Elizabeth J., ill.   II. Title.
PZ8.3.P2738 Je   2001   00-32025
                    [E]—dc21

        1 2 3 4 5 6 7 8 9 10

First Edition